Life of Fred ®

Lake

Stanley F. Schmidt, Ph.D.

Polka Dot Publishing

ISBN: 978-1-937032-26-5
Printed and bound in the United States of America
Polka Dot Publishing   Reno, Nevada

To order books in the Life of Fred series,

visit our website PolkaDotPublishing.com

Questions or comments? Email the author at lifeoffred@yahoo.com

First Printing
This book was illustrated by the author with additional clip art furnished under license from Nova
Development Corporation, which holds the copyright to that art.

Dear Parent,

At the bottom of a couple of pages I include some notes to you, the parent. They will look like this:

In this smaller size type.

They don't have to be read aloud. The notes are just between you and me to answer questions that may occur to you.

In this book in the Eden Series, we add the color red, show the difference between walking *to* a bridge and walking *on* a bridge, and point out that shouting may scare away wildlife.

Small story: Initially, there was a discussion between the author and the publisher about the title of this series.

The Eden Series vs. The Propaedeutic Series

(PRO-peh-DO-tik)

Eden won. ☺

Chapter One

We are here!
I like it.

Kingie unpacked.

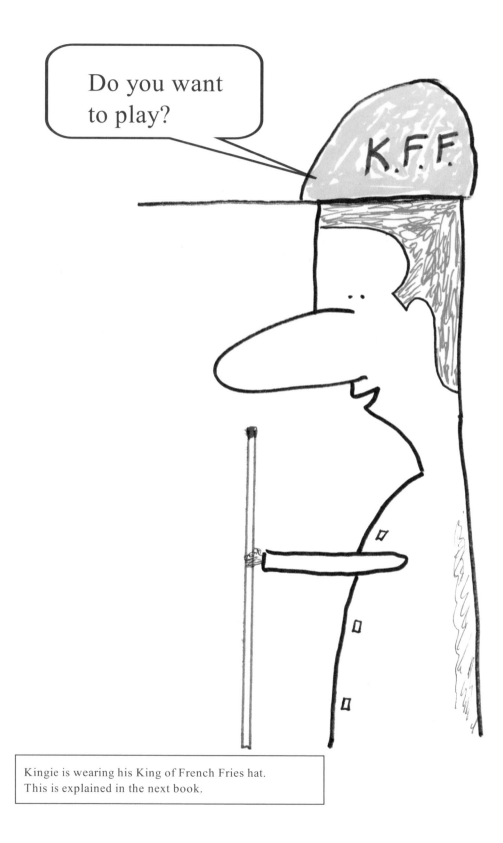

Kingie is wearing his King of French Fries hat.
This is explained in the next book.

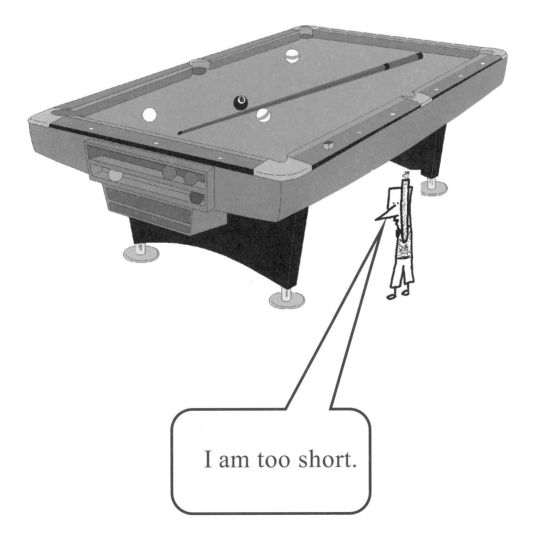

Fred had not packed food.

Kingie packed a pizza.

Fred is rarely hungry.

I see a bridge.
Will you come with me?

Chapter Two

Fred walked to the bridge.

Fred walked on the bridge.

Fred looked.

He saw a trail.

He ran back to Kingie.

Kingie was asleep.
He likes to nap after lunch.

Fred put Kingie in bed.
(Kingie had packed a bed.)

. . . while Kingie is sleeping

to the trail

This is a nice trail.

These are pretend glasses.
Fred doesn't wear glasses because he doesn't have ears.

A deer saw Fred.

Fred shouted.

The deer ran away.

Shouting at wild animals will scare them away.